KIDS CAN'T STOP READING
THE CHOOSE YOUR
OWN ADVENTURE® STORIES!

"Choose Your Own Adventure is the best thing that has come along since books themselves."
—Alysha Beyer, age 11

"I didn't read much before, but now I read my Choose Your Own Adventure books almost every night."
—Chris Brogan, age 13

"I love the control I have over what happens next."
—Kosta Efstathiou, age 17

"Choose Your Own Adventure books are so much fun to read and collect—I want them all!"
—Brendan Davin, age 11

And teachers like this series, too:
"We have read and reread, worn thin, loved, loaned, bought for others, and donated to school libraries our Choose Your Own Adventure books."

CHOOSE YOUR OWN ADVENTURE®—
AND MAKE READING MORE FUN!

CHOOSE YOUR OWN ADVENTURE®

titles in Large-Print Editions:

RETURN OF THE NINJA

BY JAY LEIBOLD

ILLUSTRATED BY FRANK BOLLE

An R.A. Montgomery Book

Gareth Stevens Publishing
MILWAUKEE

For a free color catalog describing Gareth Stevens' list of high-quality books, call 1-800-542-2595 (USA) or 1-800-461-9120 (Canada). Gareth Stevens' Fax: (414) 225-0377.

Library of Congress Cataloging-in-Publication Data available upon request from publisher.
Fax: (414) 225-0377 for the attention of the Publishing Records Department.

ISBN 0-8368-1310-3

This edition first published in 1995 by
Gareth Stevens Publishing
1555 North RiverCenter Drive, Suite 201
Milwaukee, Wisconsin 53212 USA

CHOOSE YOUR OWN ADVENTURE® is a trademark of Bantam Doubleday Dell Books for Young Readers, a division of Bantam Doubleday Dell Publishing Group, Inc.

Original conception of Edward Packard.
Interior illustrations by Frank Bolle. Cover art by Romas Kukalis.

1 2 3 4 5 6 7 8 9 99 98 97 96 95

Printed in the United States of America

RETURN OF
THE NINJA

WARNING!!!

Do not read this book straight through from beginning to end! These pages contain many different adventures that you may have as you take charge of your friend's martial arts school. From time to time as you read along, you will be asked to make a choice. Your choices will determine whether you succeed or fail in tracking down the mysterious presence at the *dojo*.

As you search for clues, you'll encounter the secret and sometimes magical world of the ninja. Your investigation may even lead you back in time! *You* are responsible for your fate because *you* make the decisions. After you make a choice, follow the instructions to see what happens to you next.

Think carefully before you make a decision. The ninja can be deadly. To find out more about them before you begin, read the Special Note on the following page. To help you in your adventures, a glossary of Eastern and martial arts terms is included.

Good luck!

SPECIAL NOTE ON THE NINJA

The ancient art of *ninjutsu* was developed in the eleventh and twelfth centuries by Japanese mountain clans. Drawing on their knowledge of martial arts, war tactics, and mystical practices—especially those practiced in a branch of Buddhism known in Japan as *shugendo*—they passed their art from one generation to the next.

Each *ryu* (tradition or school) has its own specializations and secrets, which are taught by a *sensei* (master or teacher) at the *dojo* (the place where martial arts are practiced). A student of *ninjutsu* will learn techniques of empty-hand combat, the use of weapons and special devices, as well as tactics of escape, deception, and invisibility, and the strategies of espionage, attack, and defense.

According to legend, mountain creatures called *tengu* first taught the ninja their art. They also taught them *kuji* (sorcery) and how to use mystic finger positions to channel energy, key into the underlying forces of the universe, and alter the fabric of space and time.

GLOSSARY

Aikido—*Ai*, harmony; *ki*, energy; *do*, the way. A defensive discipline using pivoting motions and the momentum of the attacker to neutralize the attack.

Dojo—The place where martial arts are practiced.

Furoshiki—A large kerchief used to tie up and carry one's belongings.

Hanbo—Ninja staff or stick.

Kaginawa—A grapple or hook attached to the end of a rope.

Kami—A spirit, demon, or deity.

Kendo—The art of sword fighting.

Kimono—A robelike garment, usually cotton or silk, worn by men and women.

Kuji—Ninja sorcery. Sometimes described as "nine hands cutting" or "nine syllables." Mystic finger positions channel energy.

Kyoketsu shoge—A rope with a steel ring on the end.

Metsubishi—Ninja blinding powder, used to temporarily cloud the vision of an opponent.

Mikkyo—Esoteric knowledge, which is the highest knowledge of all.

Ninja—A person adept at the art of *ninjutsu*.

Ninjutsu—The "art of stealth" or "way of invisibility." An unconventional discipline incorporating martial arts, special weapons, techniques of concealment, and sorcery.

Obasa—Honorary title for a grandmother.

Onshinjutsu—Specific techniques of ninja invisibility.

Rojo—House mistress, woman in charge of the
     domestic staff.
Ryu—School or tradition of martial arts.
Saiminjutsu—Ninja hypnotism.
Sakki—A kind of sixth sense or ability to detect
     harmful intentions—"the force of the
     killer."
Samurai—Japanese feudal warrior. The samurai
     were the highest class, followed by farm-
     ers, craftsmen, and finally merchants.
     Samurai were also the administrators of the
     state.
Sensei—Master, teacher.
Seppuku—Ritual suicide, an honorable form of
     death for samurai.
Shugendo—A Japanese mountain religion incor-
     porating ascetic practices and magic.
Shugenja—Mountain warrior priests or monks,
     practitioners of *shugendo*. Similar to
     Yamabushi. Some aspects of *ninjutsu* de-
     veloped out of their beliefs.
Shuko—Steel claws worn on the hands or feet.
Shuriken—A metal throwing blade, often star-
     shaped.
Tengu—Mythical creatures supposed to have first
     taught ninja their art. Sometimes portrayed
     as helpful but mischievous, other times as
     devilish, *tengu* are often shown with long
     noses or beaks, wings attached to the body
     of an old man, and long claws or finger-
     nails. They wear capes of feathers or
     leaves, live in trees in the mountains, and,
     according to one description, are the con-

densed spirit of the principle of *yin,* or darkness.

Yamabushi—Literally, "one who lies down on the mountains." A Shugendo priest, ascetic, or magician.

Yin and Yang—The polar forces of the universe, complementary opposites, whose alternation drives the processes of life.

It is a sunny, quiet spring morning when your friend Nada receives a telephone call. After she hangs up the phone, her face looks worried.

"My grandmother is very sick," she says. "It's a mysterious illness. No one can figure out what's causing it. I'm going to her house to see if I can help. Can you take charge of the *dojo* while I'm gone?"

You've been studying at Nada's *dojo* for a long time, but you're not sure if you're ready to teach the class.

"I'll do my best," you say. "I still have so much to learn myself."

"Don't worry," Nada says. "Just stick to the basics. The students need more of that anyway."

"Okay, I'll do it," you say.

"Good," Nada says. "I have to leave right away. My grandmother needs me."

Before Nada leaves, she tells you where her grandmother lives. "Her house is on a remote mountainside. There's no telephone, so I won't be able to call you. But I'll come back as soon as I can."

Nada's taxi arrives, and you wish her luck as she jumps in. "I'm sure everything will be fine," she calls out the window as the cab speeds away.

Turn to page 2.

2

Later, as you wait for the students to arrive, you think back on the events that brought you here to be a student and teacher at Nada Kurayama's family *dojo* in the mountainous Nara region of Japan.

A year has passed since you helped Nada solve the mystery of an ancient sword that had been sent to the *dojo*. The sword had terrible powers that nearly caused the destruction of the martial arts school. You and Nada discovered that, in the sixteenth century, the sword had belonged to a ninja named Sanchiro Miyamotori. He had used the sword to terrorize the countryside until, finally, he was killed by an ancestor of Nada's. Miyamotori died leaving a curse on the Kurayama family, and when the sword came to Nada's *dojo*, the *kami*—spirit—of the ninja was stirred up. You and Nada had to use all your ingenuity and martial arts skills to figure out a way to placate the angry *kami*.

During this adventure, you found out that Nada's was a ninja family that went back hundreds of years. Nada explained that she had given up *ninjutsu*, but after your adventure she began studying it again. Although you had originally come to Japan to study *aikido*, another form of martial arts, you decided to join Nada at her *dojo* and study *ninjutsu* as well.

Over the past year, you've been learning the many skills and techniques that are part of becoming a ninja. The first thing you learned from Nada is that *ninjutsu* is not like other martial arts.

Turn to page 8.

With your earplugs in, the ninja will not be able to trap you by deceiving your hearing. But you'll have to rely on your other senses, especially *sakki*—a sixth sense used to detect harmful intentions.

At first you're disoriented because your senses aren't giving you clues. You realize you must allow yourself to be receptive to the anger of the intruder.

You move through the house with silent feet, using shadow and light for concealment. As you move, you begin to feel something strange. You're picking up vibrations. The presence in the house—which you can tell is male—is like a wind on your skin.

You keep moving, drifting just out of reach of the presence, yet staying close enough that you can still feel it. Though you've seen nothing yet, you can tell the presence is getting closer. You must move faster—it's coming in on you—now it's attacking!

Turn to page 11.

4

The students begin arriving for the first exercises of the day, and you join them in the courtyard, a little nervous about taking over as teacher.

Everything goes well until late in the morning. As you're leading the class through some training drills, you happen to glance up at the roof of the house. Something catches your eye. It's just a tiny bit of black movement, no more than a flicker. It could be a bird.

In the past you might have paid no attention to such a small detail. But now, your ninja training has taught you that even the littlest thing cannot be ignored. You'll have to investigate, if only to find out you're getting too jumpy.

You begin to tell the class to carry on with their drills while you go inside. Then it occurs to you that you could have them help investigate as part of their training.

If your organize the class to help you search the house, turn to page 9.

If you think it's better not to involve the class, turn to page 86.

6

"I'm going after Nada," you say firmly. "I can't abandon her."

"I can see you are determined," Maki says. "Well, perhaps you're right. The ninja Nada is battling is very powerful and full of anger. She'll need all the help she can get. I can help you go into the past. But we should not waste any time. You must get ready immediately."

You spend the rest of the day getting ready to go back to the tenth century. There's a lot to learn about the customs and habits of the era, which are very different from the present.

At a time when Europe was in chaos and the Americas were still untouched by the sword of conquest, Japan enjoyed a flowering of its civilization in peace and tranquillity. The country was ruled by a tiny minority of the population, the Heian aristocracy. Most of them lived in the beautiful capital city of Kyoto.

The values of the era were very different from those of the violent centuries which were to follow. Delicacy of feeling and poetic expression were considered the marks of the "good persons." The aristocracy looked down upon those who were militaristic, or who came from the provinces, or did manual labor. There was no need for the samurai and their code of honor. Nor was *ninjutsu* known, except perhaps among a few mountain monks defending themselves against religious persecution.

Turn to page 61.

The march finally comes to a halt in front of the famous Bureau of Divination, also known as the Yin-Yang Bureau. There the throng begins to yell angry demands, threatening to attack. From what you can hear, they want freedom to practice their religion without persecution from the government. You recall that at this time *shugendo* was a newly evolving set of beliefs that was viewed with suspicion by conventional Buddhists.

Soon a regiment of imperial police appears and cordons off the Yin-Yang building. You edge toward the back of the crowd.

Just as you reach the back of the throng, a gang of imperial police officers appears out of nowhere and surrounds a small group of protestors—including you. Before you know what's happening, the police herd the group into a side street, cutting you off from the rest of the *shugenja*.

"Come quietly, and no one will get hurt," a captain barks at you, his sword raised.

There's no way your group can overpower the police—unless you use *ninjutsu*. You're sure that they've never seen it before, and the element of surprise might give you and the other *shugenja* a chance to break the cordon and escape.

On the other hand, if your plan doesn't work, you could be in worse trouble than you already are. You also wonder if it's wise to reveal the existence of such techniques before their time.

If you attack the police, using a ninja move, turn to page 17.

If you go quietly, turn to page 23.

8

"I know this sounds complicated," Nada told you, "but *ninjutsu* is really a very practical art. Unlike the samurai, ninja do not worry about style, or honor, or glory. We start with very basic exercises in movement and meditation, and make them part of our everyday lives. We want, after many years of study, to 'forget' our training and to achieve a state of complete emptiness which is also complete awareness and readiness."

You knew learning to become a ninja would be difficult, but you began working your way through the five stages of training, which correspond to the five elements—earth, water, fire, wind, and the Void. First you became familiar with your own physical capabilities and limits. Then you learned how to deal with an attacker, and how to enter the flow of a conflict and see yourself and your enemy as inseparable parts of a whole. Finally, you attempted to put yourself in the center of danger without fear, where you could change the appearance of a situation so that what seemed to be weakness became strength. Along the way, you learned the ninja techniques of stealth and invisibility, including methods of escape, concealment, and disappearing. You practiced empty-hand combat and self-defense, methods of jumping and climbing, and the arts of spying and strategy.

You have yet to reach the final level, the Void, in which you leave behind your training. "Some day," Nada told you, "you will learn *mikkyo*, or esoteric knowledge. Esoteric knowledge is the highest knowledge of all."

Turn to page 4.

Clapping your hands to get the class's attention, you announce, "We're going to put some of our training to work. An intruder may have entered the house. We're going to make a thorough search of it."

You divide the class into groups, giving each group a part of the house to search. Taking four students with you, you circle around to the back of the house where you think you'd be most likely to catch an intruder.

Before you open the door, you ask the students which one of the five different ways of approaching danger you should take.

"The fire approach," a student named Basho says. "Let's set a trap."

"I would have thought the water approach would be better," you say. "That way we can dodge an attack."

"But we might let the intruder get away," Basho responds.

You wonder if you should let Basho have his way and take the more aggressive fire approach, rather than the defensive water approach.

If you accept Basho's suggestion to set up a trap, turn to page 76.

If you decide to take a defensive approach, turn to page 12.

In a flash you crouch and roll sideways, opening a secret compartment in a chest that stands upright against the wall. At the same moment, an object— probably a deadly *shuriken*—thunks into the wood of the chest.

Inside the chest, you open another secret door into a hidden passage behind the wall. For all the intruder can tell, you've just disappeared. You remove the earplugs, and through the wall, you hear a grunt of frustration.

You wait in tense silence for his next move. He leaves the room. You go down the hidden passage to a spot where you can hear anything in the house.

A few moments later, you hear sounds coming from one of the storerooms in the basement. Hurrying down a passage in that direction, you hear loud crashing sounds, as if the storeroom's being torn apart.

When you get there, the sounds have stopped. Cautiously you push open a secret panel that lets you into the storeroom. The contents of the room are strewn about in chaos. You rush out after the intruder, but already you can sense that he has gone.

Turn to page 14.

12

"I think we'd better be more defensive," you say to Basho. "Let's use the water approach to search the house."

One by one you and the four students slip into the house, moving with careful stealth, always listening for sounds that might give an intruder away. A slow and thorough search of the house reveals nothing. Still you can't shake the feeling that someone has been there.

Back in the courtyard of the *dojo*, the other groups of students report that they found nothing, either. Deciding there isn't anything else you can do, you resume the training drills.

For the rest of the day you're occupied with your classes. By the time you send the students home, you're tired from the long day of teaching.

Alone in the house you begin to prepare your dinner. Thinking back on the flicker of movement you thought you saw, you wonder if maybe you were just nervous about being in charge of the *dojo* for the first time. You decide to forget about the incident.

Turn to page 16.

You thank Sakai, and help Nada hobble toward the stairs. Finally you reach the door and take Nada out to the garden, where you find a secluded spot to rest. Nada slowly returns to herself. "Are you ready to return to the present?" you ask.

Somehow Nada finds the strength to put you into a trance and take both of you back to the *dojo*.

A couple of days later, while Nada is at her grandmother's being nursed back to health, she tells you what happened. "When the ninja and I went into the past, we discovered that his story was at least partly accurate. Mito Hitari was to be exiled for plotting to assassinate his brother Taro."

You then tell Nada how you met Sakai, after achieving fame as a teacher of *ninjutsu,* and how he confirmed that Mito's intentions were evil. "According to Sakai, Mito was simply envious of his brother."

"Well," Nada goes on, "instead of accepting this, the ninja became more enraged, and he took it out on me. I had no choice but to fight him in the garden. I'd felt I would lose, and I was right. That's the last thing I remembered until you came and rescued me."

"You did well," Nada's grandmother says to you. "But you also made a grave mistake. You should not have introduced ideas such as *ninjutsu* before their time. We can only hope that what you taught will fade out among the *shugenja* before any damage is done."

You will never know whether your decision changed the course of history.

The End

14

You go back to the storeroom and try to put things in order. Nothing seems to be missing. You wonder what he was after.

You're unsure what to do next. If you go to Nada's grandmother's house, you'll have to leave the *dojo* unguarded. You go to bed, deciding it can wait until morning.

But you never have to make a choice. Sleeping fitfully, as a part of you is on watch all night, you're woken by a knock on the door.

"I am Maki, Nada's grandmother," a small, steely-haired woman says. "We've got problems."

"Come in *Obasa*," you say.

You prepare some morning tea, but before you can tell Maki about last night, she launches into her own story. "A ninja came bursting into my house around midnight. He demanded we give him a sword. Of course we didn't know what he was talking about. Then Nada realized he wanted the sword that was sent to the *dojo* last year—the one that caused you and her so much trouble."

"So that's what it was," you interrupt. "An intruder broke in here last night and made a mess of the storeroom. It must have been the ninja, looking for the sword. When he didn't find it, he went to your house. But—I thought you were sick."

"I was," she replies, "but Nada figured out that I was being poisoned. Not only that, it was a ninja poison. Luckily she knew how to counteract it."

"So your poisoning was probably a ploy to draw Nada away from the *dojo*," you say.

"Without a doubt," Maki agrees.

Turn to page 18.

16

As darkness falls, you begin to feel the emptiness of the house. Every little sound seems magnified. You can't help feeling that there's something odd about the silence.

Then, just as you finish eating, you hear a small but distinct sound from the other side of the house. For a moment, you want only to run away. Then you remind yourself that you're responsible for the safety of the *dojo*, and that you're also a ninja in training—it's time to use your knowledge.

Though it seems odd, you realize that the first thing you must do is meditate, in order to clear your mind for whatever is ahead. So, in spite of your racing adrenaline, you sit cross-legged, close your eyes, and begin breathing slowly.

As you enter a state of deeper listening, you're immediately aware that there *is* a presence in the house, and it's no ordinary intruder. It's a very strong presence, perhaps even a ninja.

Just then, a sound comes from the opposite side of the house. Then another from the roof.

Your eyes pop open. It's time to act—but where should you begin? You wonder if there is more than one person. You also remember that ninja can use sound vibrations to fool their prey. The noises might be traps set for you. You wonder if you'd be better off not to count on your sense of hearing—maybe you should even cut off your hearing altogether, by using earplugs.

If you decide to use earplugs, turn to page 3.

If you decide not to use earplugs and use all your senses, turn to page 112.

You start your attack by throwing a handful of *metsubishi,* or blinding powder, into the eyes of the police officer nearest you. Then, grabbing the staff of one of your fellow prisoners, you use it as a ninja *hanbo* to knock down the next two officers who come at you, one with each end of the staff.

Now the other *shugenja* join in the fray, and there is confusion. A police officer grabs your *hanbo* from behind. You twist under him and use the *hanbo* to flip him over your back. This gives you an opening to escape, and you take off down the side street.

To your surprise, the rest of the *shugenja* follow once they get free of the police officers. All of you run until you think you've put enough distance between yourselves and the police.

"*Sensei,*" one of the monks says to you, using a term of respect, "if not for you we would surely have ended up in the emperor's dungeon."

You're taken aback at being called a *sensei*— but then you realize that the monks have probably never seen anything like what you just did. "I was just trying to help," you say modestly.

"You must come back to our monastery with us," another monk says. "We will show you our hospitality and properly express our gratitude. Perhaps you can tell us how you gained your powers." The others in the circle nod in agreement.

It's a delicate situation. You may give grave offense by refusing their offer. Besides, they may be able to help you. And if you stay in Kyoto, you risk capture by the police.

Turn to page 24.

18

"Who is this ninja?" you ask.

"It was hard to tell, he was babbling so," Maki says. "But from what I could understand, his name is Hitari, and somehow he's related to the Miyamotori family. He kept talking about how the sword was his rightful inheritance, and he was going to avenge his family honor."

"What happened to his family honor?"

"It seems that a thousand years ago, his ancestor Mito Hitari was sent into exile for trying to kill his brother Taro. Mito's brother later started what became the Miyamotori branch of the family. Hitari claimed that his ancestor was wrongly exiled, and that by getting the sword he would restore the Hitari family's rightful place."

"Did Nada tell him the sword is gone?"

"She certainly tried to." Maki sighs. "But he wouldn't believe her. He said she wanted to steal his powers, and she had the sword hidden somewhere."

"So—where are they now?"

"Well," Maki replies, "that's hard to say. Nada and Hitari became locked in a contest of wills. I wasn't yet strong enough to help Nada at the time. The battle moved outside, in the woods, where, from what I could hear, it went on most of the night."

Go on to the next page.

Maki pauses before continuing, "This may sound strange, but I know you will understand from your previous adventures with Nada. I believe the battle entered the time dimension. It became so intense that they broke out of this time and place, and went back to a time a thousand years ago, when Hitari's ancestor lived."

"Then I must go back there and help Nada," you say.

"It is dangerous," Maki protests. "You do not know enough. If you don't find her, you may be stranded in the past."

"There are risks in either case," Maki says. "The choice is yours to make."

If you insist on going into the past to find Nada, turn to page 6.

If you agree with Maki that it's wiser not to, turn to page 26.

20

Late in the evening everything is ready for you to leave, disguised as a monk. You sit down with Maki. She directs you in a series of meditations, focusing in on Nada and where in the weave of history she is. Maki intones the syllables of *kuji*, whose vibrations help open the fabric of time. You fall into a trance as Maki puts you under the spell of *saiminjutsu.*

When you return to consciousness, different sensations hit you at once. You realize you're on a steep mountainside. The rumble of feet and a frightening, relentless chant is coming from just above you. When you look up, the glare of rushing torches hurts your eyes.

You think it's strange that Buddhist priests are carrying all sorts of weapons. But when you see their long hair, you realize that these are not just priests, they're *shugenja*—mountain warrior priests, precursors of the ninja.

You blend in with the crowd as you're swept up. The horde of priests rumbles down the narrow mountain path. Soon a city appears below, and when you get a glimpse of the magnificent build-ings, you realize it's Kyoto. The priests must be on some sort of a raid. You don't want to give yourself away, so you just go along with them.

The stampede barges past the terrified guards at one of the gates of the city, and continues up a wide avenue. You're surprised to find that you're headed for the northern part of the city, where the imperial palace and government offices are. You begin to wonder what you've gotten yourself into.

Turn to page 7.

"How do I find Sakai?" you ask.

"Go up the road and take the right fork around to the other side of the mountain. After you cross the waterfall, there will be a small trail leading up the valley. Follow it, and where it bends to the right, you will see Sakai's hut."

You gather up your *furoshiki,* and set off up the road. Finally, at daybreak, you find the track up to Sakai's house. You find Sakai, a small, somber man, engrossed in his morning rituals. You introduce yourself, and explain who sent you. "I understand you are in the service of Mito Hitari," you say.

Sakai looks suspicious, so you explain, "I'm looking for a friend."

Sakai looks you over, then invites you into his hut. Once you convince him you're not a friend of the Hitari, he begins to talk.

"Mito Hitari enlisted me to help him. He told me that his brother Taro had betrayed him. I performed many kinds of sorcery against Taro, but none of them worked. It is because Mito's intentions are bad. He is envious of his brother."

"Have you told him this?"

"It would be the end of me. He is too powerful. And Taro would have me imprisoned for practicing sorcery against him. But what about your friend?"

"Her name is Nada," you say. "I think she's engaged in a fight with one of the Hitari."

"I can take you to Mito's house," Sakai offers. "I will say you are my student. No one will suspect you are looking for Nada."

Turn to page 29.

You put up no resistance, and the police take you and the *shugenja* to the imperial prison. They put each of you into a separate cell, where you spend the rest of the night. You don't want to call attention to yourself, so you ask no questions.

In the morning your hands are bound, and you're taken to the Yin-Yang Bureau. You're set before a Buddhist priest, who looks down sternly at you.

"You were caught disturbing the peace and violating the sacred grounds of the Bureau of Divination. What is the purpose of this outrage?"

"I don't know," you say innocently. "You see, I just arrived from a remote province in Hokkaido. I am a pilgrim. I know little of these matters. I came here to learn—"

"And what are your religious practices in Hokkaido?"

You know you can't show any hesitation. You blurt out some ninja philosophy, knowing it will sound strange to him.

The priest regards you for several minutes with expressionless eyes. Finally he says, "It may be that you are telling the truth. You have a very strange way of speaking, and your philosophy is unfamiliar to me. Indeed, everything about you is peculiar. Nevertheless, you have committed a grave offense. I will have to speak to the emperor about you."

With that you're dismissed and taken back to your cell.

Turn to page 33.

24

You hike back up the mountain, surrounded by your new devotees. They're full of questions about your strange features and accent. You answer them as best you can, saying you're from a far away province in Hokkaido. You hope no one is familiar with the region. Most of the *shugenja* seem happy to believe whatever you say.

"But, *sensei*," one of the monks says impatiently, "what we really want to know is how you learned your powers. Will you teach us?"

You ponder for a moment. The simplest thing to do might be to tell them about the new art of *ninjutsu*, pretending that it has been developed by the monks in your province. It would create goodwill among the *shugenja*, and convince them of your importance. Perhaps then they would help you find Nada.

But you also wonder if it's right to introduce these new ideas before their time. You could claim you're pledged to secrecy, refuse to talk, and hope they'll still be willing to help you find Nada.

If you decide to tell the shugenja *about* ninjutsu, *turn to page 34.*

If you say you can't teach them, turn to page 56.

26

"I guess you're right," you say to Maki. "It's too dangerous to go into the past. What can we do instead?"

Maki rubs her chin. "Well . . . we can meditate and send out *kuji* to Nada, to make her stronger. And we can be prepared to help her when she and the ninja return."

For the next three days, you and Maki keep a vigil, hoping your meditations and *kuji* reach Nada. The hours stretch on endlessly as you wait for something to happen. Nothing does.

Then, on the fourth morning, Maki comes in and wakes you up before dawn. Her face is sad. "I had a dream," she says. "I'm afraid Nada won't be coming back."

You put your face in your hands. "I should have gone to help her."

"It is not your fault," Maki says gently. "Better that one of you, at least, is still here to run the *dojo*."

The End

"That's not important—do you want to meet with me or not?" you ask the ninja.

"I'll meet you," the ninja says. "But if you try anything, Yoshi will suffer for it."

"It's a deal," you say. "Where do we meet?"

"Go to the village of Kanayama. There is a public phone at the post office. It will ring at three o'clock this afternoon."

"I'll be there," you promise, and hang up.

"This is foolish," Detective Jonsuro starts, but you interrupt him. "I think I can convince the ninja we don't have the sword," you say. "I began to hear some doubt in his voice."

"We don't have much time to get to Kanayama," Nada says. "Let's go."

"I guess I can't stop you," the detective says with resignation, "so I'll give you a ride."

Jonsuro speeds up to Kanayama. You make him let you out short of the village so you can walk into the post office alone. Precisely at three the phone rings.

"Walk directly north out of the post office," a voice says. "You will find a path leading up the mountain ridge. Follow it."

Turn to page 97.

Sakai leads you on a secret path down the mountain and into Kyoto. It takes most of the day to get to the Hitari house, but finally the two of you arrive at the front door. Sakai is greeted by the *rojo*.

"This is my disciple," Sakai tells her, introducing you. "There is no need to tell the master I am here, yet. I must attend to other business first."

The *rojo* bows and lets you in. You follow Sakai into the mansion, until finally he says, "Wait here. I will make some inquiries."

Half an hour later Sakai returns. "There is talk of a prisoner in the cellar," he whispers. "No one knows who it is or why the prisoner is there. They say a distant Hitari cousin just arrived from the provinces, and he is responsible for the prisoner. There were sounds of a fight last night."

"Can we find the prisoner?"

Sakai checks to make sure no one is around. "Perhaps," he says. "Follow me."

You sneak through a small door that leads to a narrow set of stone steps. The steps descend into a complex of dank cellars. In one of the cellars, you find an unconscious figure curled up in a corner.

Turning the figure over, you barely recognize Nada. Her face is swollen and bruised. She slowly opens her eyes as you shake her. You can't tell if she recognizes you. You untie the ropes around her wrists and ankles and help her to her feet. "How do we get out of here?" you ask Sakai.

"The same way we came in," he replies. "But you are on your own now. I cannot risk being caught with you."

Turn to page 13.

To have more space for your ninja demonstration, you move into the middle of the room. You take deep breaths and flex your knees before you begin. The attendants stand back. With a shout, you do a back flip, and then a blinding series of punches and strikes, ending with a triple backward handspring.

Panting, you bow to the emperor after your performance. His face looks stricken. The attendants shrink away from you. You look at the emperor, waiting for his reaction.

"Yes," he finally manages to say in a restrained voice, "that was highly unusual." He motions quickly for you to be taken from the room.

The guards lead you back to your cell. A short while later, the priest comes to fetch you. "We are moving you to the Divination Bureau, where we can keep an eye on you," he says. "The emperor was quite horrified by your demonstration. He said he has never seen anything so vulgar and violent. He thinks you must be a very dangerous person, and he is concerned that this art not be spread throughout the country."

You're taken to the Yin-Yang Bureau under heavy guard. As they lock you up, you reflect dejectedly on how difficult it will be to escape.

The End

You know you don't have long to come up with some lines of poetry. The ability to recite quickly is considered a mark of a "good person."

"To forget your intention," you recite, "and let it flow together with thought and action, is to achieve the highest state of unthinking."

The emperor says nothing, and you wonder if you should go on. But then he comments, "I have never heard such ideas before. And you went right to the essence of the matter. Very thought-provoking."

He does seem lost in thought for a while, before he says, "Tell me more."

You begin to expound on your philosophy, starting slowly. But as the emperor repeatedly says, "Very interesting," you gain confidence and speak more freely.

Finally, after two hours, the emperor grows tired. "This has been most intriguing," he says. "You please me. You must tell me if there is anything we can do to make your visit more pleasant."

"Actually," you speak up boldly, "there is. I came to Kyoto with a friend, but we've been separated. She is named Nada. In fact, she is my teacher."

"Hmm," the emperor muses, "I do believe there was a recent report of a visitor of that description. At the Hitari house, as I recall."

Your heart jumps when you hear this. The emperor calls an attendant to his side and begins giving instructions. You are led from the chamber, your audience with the emperor at a close.

Turn to page 47.

The next morning the priest shows up at your cell. "The emperor is curious," he says simply. "He will see you now."

You're escorted to the imperial palace. You're surprised at the simplicity of the grounds and of the emperor's residence, which is located in the innermost part of the Nine-Fold Enclosure. Pausing before the doors to the emperor's chamber, the priest murmurs, "Your fate will probably be determined by the impression you make upon the emperor." With that he turns and leaves.

The emperor's chamber also seems unassuming. There is little color or ornamentation, and the only furniture is a small chair in which the emperor is seated. He is young, perhaps your age, with a smooth, fresh face. His features are fine, and there's a delicacy and grace about the way he moves.

You make your bow of homage, a slow, formal bow as far down as you can go. The emperor motions the guards to unbind your hands and leave the room.

"So," he says in a soft voice, "tell me about yourself."

Turn to page 40.

34

You launch into a lecture on the art of *ninjutsu*. Your audience listens with rapt attention. Even after you reach the mountain monastery, they keep you talking late into the night.

Word of your exploits and teachings spreads quickly. You gain instant fame among the mountain *shugenja*. All through the next day, monks arrive to hear you speak. You're flooded with students, so many that it is impossible to escape them. You're a prisoner of your own success.

Finally, at the evening meal, exhausted from answering questions all day, you ask for something in return. "I need some help," you say. "I traveled here with my teacher. But we've been separated, and I must find her. She may be at the Hitari house."

One of the *shugenja* hesitates before asking, "Which Hitari?"

"I believe his name is Mito," you reply.

"Mito is feuding with his brother Taro," the *shugenja* explains. "It all started when Taro was raised to the third rank, while Mito remained on the fourth. He is jealous of his brother." The *shugenja* confers with his friends before going on. "We know a monk named Sakai who has been enlisted by Mito to help him overthrow his brother."

"Could I speak to Sakai?" you ask.

Go on to the next page.

"Of course," the *shugenja* replies. "He lives on the other side of the mountain. I will send for him."

Just then a breathless messenger arrives from the city. "The Yin-Yang Bureau has gotten wind of the new teacher. A regiment of imperial guards is on its way to arrest us all!"

"You must go," the *shugenja* tells you. "You can find Sakai's hut by yourself."

"No," you say, "I will stay and help you."

"You have helped us enough," he says. "You must look for your friend."

Maybe the *shugenja* is right—maybe you should go find Sakai. But he lives on the other side of the mountain, farther away from Kyoto. Besides, the monks may need you here.

If you try to find Sakai, turn to page 22.

If you stay with the shugenja, *turn to page 48.*

36

You jump off the wall into the Hitari garden and wait for dawn to come. There you change into clothes that will allow you to pass as a house servant, and slip into the house through a side window.

For a while you prowl through the house, listening, but you don't hear much. A few members of the staff give you questioning looks, but you just hurry by. Finally your sharp ears pick up voices coming from a few rooms away. You glide silently among the screens that serve as walls in the house, until you can hear every word that is being said from behind one of the screens.

"But you can't just kill him!" a man is saying. "Everyone would know you ordered it. Besides, it would be very difficult."

"I must," another man says in a low voice full of anger. "For too long my brother has acted superior to me. For him to be promoted to the third rank, while I stay at the fourth, is the final outrage."

"Beg pardon, Lord Mito," the first man says soothingly, "but perhaps we should give our *shugenja's* sorcery a chance to work." (You know that a *shugenja* is a religious sorceror.)

"He's had his chance," Mito says.

"But we must at least wait for some pretext for action—" the other pleads.

"I need no pretext!" Mito hisses. "I shall do as I want."

Just then you hear movement from somewhere nearby. Mito hears it, too. "What's that?" he says.

"I'll look," the other man says.

Turn to page 44.

The ninja stands up and shakes your hand. "Yoshi will be waiting for you at the post office," he says. "You will understand if I don't stay here any longer."

He turns and leaves, and you run back down the mountain path. Yoshi is waiting at the post office, as promised, and you take him back to Jonsuro and Nada for a happy reunion.

The End

You spot a good place to scale the wall, which, when you get up close, you see is only about six feet high. You stand back, get a good run at it, and, placing your feet against the wall, use your momentum to walk far enough up the wall to grab on to the top. You drop down on the other side and you're in the city.

From the look of the crumbling buildings and vacant lots, you think you must be in the western part of Kyoto, which you remember has seen many fires, and has gradually become more and more deserted over the years.

You wander through the eerily empty streets. A man stealing down a side street catches your eye. Cutting through an abandoned house, you intercept him at the next corner.

"Where is the Hitari house?" you blurt from a recess of the abandoned house.

The man jumps back when he hears your voice. "Did you say Hitari?"

"Yes, I'm looking for the residence of Mito Hitari."

He looks nervously at you. "Ah, I don't believe I know it," he says, and runs off.

There's something strange about the way he answered you. Thinking he may know more than he claims, you decide to follow him.

Using ninja techniques of stealth, you shadow the man through the streets of Kyoto. He never knows you are there.

Turn to page 46.

40

"Your Excellency," you stutter, "I come from a place far, far away, high in the mountains, whose cold and snow are far from civilization. I have come to your great city seeking wisdom."

A smile plays on his lips. "Tell me," he says, "do all the people from your region look as strange as you?"

"More or less," you reply uncertainly.

He seems amused by this. "More or less!" he says, clapping his hands. "What a charming answer."

You smile, unsure what he finds so charming. The subtle scent of his perfume wafts over you.

"Now," he says, smoothing his robes, "I understand you have some very unusual beliefs. Give me a demonstration. Show me an example of your art."

You wonder how to impress the emperor. Should you show him a series of ninja moves, maybe a back flip and succession of kicks, punches, and handsprings? He's probably never seen anything like that. Or should you try instead to make up some lines of ninja philosophy about the poetry inherent in movement?

The emperor waits expectantly.

---

*If you attempt to do the ninja moves,
turn to page 30.*

If you try to recite the poetry, turn to page 31.

"There they are!" someone cries. You and Nada heave the ninja down the corridor and into the path of five of the household staff coming at you. Then you dash back through the house, leading Nada to the window where you came in.

"It sounds like the entire household is after us," Nada comments as she swings out the window and into the tree. You follow, and as you jump down onto the wall, people are yelling at you from the window.

"Which way?" Nada says. "They'll have every way out of the garden closed off."

"I know where we can go," you say. You jump down into the garden next door, and take her to the lighted window you remember from earlier in the night. You knock on the partition, then open it and fall inside, where you find the man you followed engaged in deep conversation with his girlfriend.

Nada follows, and you quickly close the partition. You put your finger to your lips, and say, "We won't stay long—just until the fuss is over."

Turn to page 103.

42

You wrap a length of rope you still have in your pocket around the trunk of a tree, and use the rope to lean out and brace yourself while you walk, foot over foot, up the tree.

For a while everything is silent. You wait, knowing that patience is the best—and only—strategy you have.

Suddenly you hear Nada calling to you from the house, but you can't make out what she's saying. You don't want to give away your position by answering, but then you remember a trick you learned from her. You call back, but project your voice so that it sounds as if it's coming from the edge of the rock face.

Still you wait. You think Nada and the ninja must both be moving toward that spot, but neither makes a sound.

Then you see the ninja—below you, right at the edge of the rocks. You plan your leap carefully. You jump from the high tree into a smaller sapling that's between you and the ninja. The sapling bends with your weight, nearly to the ground, close enough to where you can hit the ninja squarely with a double-footed kick.

He never sees the blow coming. The kick knocks him to the edge of the rocks, where he desperately claws for a hold. He doesn't find one. With a scream he tumbles down the rock face.

Nada arrives a moment later. You both look over the edge of the rocks. There's no sign of life. "That must be the end of him," Nada says. "It's too bad we'll never find out what this was all about."

Turn to page 88.

You put the sword on the ground and slowly let go of it, watching as the ninja motions to his man to let go of Yoshi.

"Run, Yoshi!" you cry.

Yoshi bolts into the woods, and, leaving the sword, you follow him. As you do, you see the ninja jump greedily to the sword.

"They're not chasing us," Yoshi says, looking over his shoulder.

You push him to keep running. "They will be when they figure out the sword is a phony."

You and Yoshi have enough of a head start that you make it back to the village, where Nada and Detective Jonsuro are waiting for you in the post office. Nada hugs Yoshi. Jonsuro is tracking the homing device on a map, and sends a detachment of police out after the ninja.

Later Yoshi is able to fill you in on why he was kidnapped. "The ninja said his family is a branch of the family that originally owned the sword. About a thousand years ago, his ancestor was sent into exile. All these years, his part of the family hasn't been able to restore their honor, but he thought by getting the sword he could start a powerful ninja *ryu,* a training school of his own. I guess he was going to use the school to get revenge."

"Well," Nada says, "that sword won't get him very far."

Although Jonsuro's men don't find the ninja, they do find the sword in the woods. Did the ninja discover it was a fake? You never know, because you never hear from the ninja again.

The End

Slipping away before Mito and his advisor catch you, you hurry to the back of the house. You go through a sliding door into the garden and stop to think for a moment. From what you've overheard, Mito is plotting to kill his brother, which must be the reason he will eventually be exiled.

As soon as you turn the corner around a hedge, into a small clearing by a pond, you see them—Nada and the ninja faced off against each other. Nada sees you immediately, and gestures to the ninja to wait, saying, "It's one of the servants."

The ninja turns and waits for you to approach, keeping his eye on Nada at the same time. You play your part. "Pardon me," you say meekly, drawing close to the ninja, "but Lord Mito—"

Before you finish your sentence, your arm strikes out, smashing the ninja on the neck. He crumples to the ground.

"Am I glad you came along," Nada says with a sigh of relief. "He insisted on fighting. I don't think I could have handled him alone."

You tell Nada what you just overheard in the house. "We were eavesdropping on the conversation, too," she says. "But instead of convincing Hitari that his ancestor would be sent into exile for good reasons, it only made him more angry, and he insisted we fight it out."

You look down at Hitari. "What should we do about him?"

"He'll be taken care of by Lord Mito," Nada replies, "Let's leave him here and get back to our own time before anyone else comes out."

The End

46

You follow the man into the wealthy eastern section of the city. He goes around to the back of one of these houses and slips through a hedge into a large garden. You see that he's headed for a lighted window at the back of the house.

You race around the other side of some bushes, and cut him off before he reaches the window.

"I won't hurt you," you say, stepping up to him in a slightly threatening way. "Just tell me where the Hitari house is."

He nods over to your left. "It's on the other side of that wall. But please," he says, grabbing your sleeve, "don't tell them you saw me here."

Hoping he has information, you say, "Why not?"

"A cousin of the Hitari lives there," he says shyly, "and I am in love with her. But since I am below her station, they will kill me if they find out I am seeing her."

"Don't worry," you assure him, and disappear into the garden. You find the wall, and use your *kaginawa* to climb it.

From the top of the wall, you eye the dark, heavy Hitari house and think about how to get in. Should you sneak in wearing dark ninja clothes right now? Or should you wait until morning to disguise yourself as a servant, so that you can move freely through the house?

If you decide to enter the Hitari house now, dressed as a ninja, turn to page 53.

If you decide to wait until morning, turn to page 36.

You're taken to a small room in the palace, where an attendant tells you to wait.

You sit on the floor. Every once in a while you're brought tea and food. The hours drag by. Finally you hear voices approaching. An attendant announces that you have a visitor.

"Nada!" you cry.

She rushes to greet you. "What are you doing here?"

"Can't you see that I'm a guest of the emperor?" you exclaim. Once the attendant has left, you explain how you came into the past to help her.

"Well," Nada says, "you arrived just in time. The emperor's men just barely saved me from a fight with Hitari—a fight I think I would have lost."

"So what was all this about?"

"Hitari wanted the sword," Nada answers. "He thought he could use it to start a ninja *ryu*. This would help him restore the honor his family lost when his ancestor Mito was exiled in this time. But when Hitari and I got here, we saw that Mito truly did deserve his punishment—he was jealous of his brother and was plotting to kill him."

"Then why were you and Hitari about to fight?"

"Hitari couldn't accept the truth when he saw it. He turned his anger on me. But this is the nature of jealousy. He was infected by the spirit of his ancestor."

"Well, before he comes after us again," you say, "let's get out of here and get back to the present as fast as we can."

The End

48

"I'm staying here," you insist. "I can't abandon you."

The *shugenja* protest your decision. But soon there's no time for arguing as the first of the imperial regiment arrives. You hear yells and the clash of metal on metal. The guards are trying to push into the monastery. You rush to the door with the other *shugenja* in time to hear the guards' captain saying, "We only want the newcomer. There is no need to fight!"

People are running everywhere as the guards break through to the inside. There is hand-to-hand fighting all around you. You use kicks and punches to flatten several surprised guards. But more and more come pouring in, and finally there are too many for you to handle. They pin you down and drag you outside. Some of the *shugenja* chase after, trying to free you, but the guards are too strong for them.

As you're shackled and taken back toward Kyoto, you smell smoke. You look back to see the monastery in flames.

You're quickly brought to trial at the Imperial Court, and condemned to life in prison. Because of your legendary powers, you're under heavy guard twenty-four hours a day. Escape will be next to impossible. But you have a lifetime to try.

The End

50

Once you've put together everything you'll need to appear as a tenth-century carpenter, Maki sits down with you. Using *saiminjutsu,* she puts you into a trance, and then begins the *kuji* hand-signs that will part the weave of time for you.

When you open your eyes, you're on a mountainside. A noise is coming down the mountain toward you. You scramble out of the way just as a mass of robed monks, carrying torches and all kinds of weapons, rumbles by, chanting angrily. You realize they're probably *shugenja*—warrior priests—on a raid.

You wait until the road is clear to venture out, and follow the road down the mountain through a moonlit forest. As you near the bottom, a view of a beautiful city opens before you. It is Kyoto.

The city is surrounded by a wall, and there are eighteen gates. You wonder if you'll be able to get through a gate at this time of night. You could wait until morning, when the gatekeepers will be less suspicious. Or, you could try to get into the city tonight by scaling the wall.

If you try to scale the wall now,
turn to page 39.

If you decide it's better to go through a gate
in the morning, turn to page 54.

"Here is what we must do," Maki instructs. "I will tell him that the sword no longer exists. Then I will try to exorcise the *kami*. But you will have to leave us alone for a while."

Several hours later, you and Nada return to the room to find the ninja asleep. Maki has untied him.

"He will wake up in a few hours," she says.

"How did it go?" you ask.

Maki tries to be modest, but her pride shows through. "The exorcism worked," she says, "and he also understands that the sword is gone. I found out that he is a descendant of Mito Hitari. A thousand years ago Mito was sent into exile for trying to kill his brother, of whom he was jealous. As we know, the curse of envy is that your spirit remains envious long after you have gone."

"And that was the spirit that possessed him?" you ask.

"Yes," Maki says.

"Where does the sword come in?" Nada asks.

"The Hitari are a branch of the Miyamotori family," Maki answers. "When the ninja heard about the sword, he became convinced that it could be the keystone for his *ryu*. Through the *ryu*, he thought he could restore his family's honor. But now he understands he can start the *ryu* without the sword, and that he must let the past be. He was very apologetic about what he did to you and Nada."

"Well," you say with a smile, "I guess Nada and I can let the past be, too."

The End

Still perched on the top of the wall, you dig through your *furoshiki* and quickly change into black ninja clothes that will enable you to blend in with the shadows. You climb a tree that enables you to reach a gable of the house. Swinging hand over hand on the gable, you get your foot onto a window ledge, and pull yourself in.

Staying low and using the shadows, you steal through the rooms, stopping in each to listen. Still you hear nothing—so you're stunned when you turn a corner and knock heads with another ninja!

He immediately attacks, grabbing your neck to pinch the vital nerve that will leave you unconscious. But someone from behind kicks the ninja's feet out from under him. He falls to the floor, dragging you with him. You roll out of his grip as he uses his elbows to knock whoever is behind him so hard that the person crashes through a screen. That gives you the chance to grab the ninja's arm and throw him to the ground, but he uses his momentum to pull you along and flings you into another screen. You hear wood splintering.

As you clear your head, the ninja comes at you again. But suddenly the other person comes flying out of nowhere—and now you see that it's Nada! She knocks the ninja down, but he gets her in an arm lock. You draw out your *kaginawa* and wrap it under the ninja's arms and over the back of his neck. This frees Nada, who helps you use the *kaginawa* to tie him up.

Meanwhile, you hear shouts throughout the house, and footsteps coming your way.

Turn to page 41.

54

At daylight you approach a gate to the city. The guards ask you all kinds of questions about where you're from and who you're going to work for, which makes you a little more nervous about your disguise as a carpenter. But you answer with confidence, and they let you in.

You walk down one of the wide avenues of the city, marveling at the mansions of the aristocracy. From behind you, voices order you to stand aside. You turn and watch an ornate ox-drawn carriage go plodding by very slowly, the nobleman inside scanning the passing scene. You try to stand out of the way, but he spots you. He orders one of his servants to bring you over to talk to him.

"Are you a carpenter?" he asks, eyeing your tools.

"Yes, my lord," you reply. Seizing a chance for information, you continue, "I am looking for the Hitari household. They want me to do a job for them."

"That's very good, but I need some repairs done on my mansion first. You'll come along with me." He closes his curtain before you can reply. His servants grab your sleeve, and you have no choice but to follow along behind the nobleman's carriage.

Turn to page 94.

"Hello, police?" you say into the telephone. "I've caught someone breaking into my house. Could you send an officer over right away?"

Five minutes later a pair of police officers arrive. They see the ninja unconscious on the floor, and eye you suspiciously.

You tell them the whole story, from when you saw movement on the roof to how your students helped capture the intruder. "I guess you have enough witnesses," one of the officers says. "But be sure you're available for questioning."

"I will," you promise as they load the unconscious body into their car.

The next day you read in the newspaper about a ninja escaping from the local jail.

Nada returns in the afternoon. After you've told her what happened while she was away, she says, "When I arrived at my grandmother's I found out that she was sick because she was being slowly poisoned. It was a ninja poison. Once I figured that out, I knew what antidote to give her."

"So what probably happened was that the ninja poisoned your grandmother to draw you away from the *dojo*," you reason. "Then yesterday he broke in."

"I think you're right," Nada says. "But what's the purpose behind all of this?"

"I don't know," you say, "but I think we should be ready for the ninja's next move."

But his next move never comes. There's no sign of the ninja after that, and you're at a loss to explain the incident.

The End

56

"I'm sorry, I can't teach you," you say to the shugenja. "The sensei who taught me pledged me to secrecy. I can tell you no more."

The shugenja seem disappointed, though they understand. "It is too bad," one says. "If you did choose to be a teacher, you would have many students. Nevertheless, you must be our guest at the monastery."

After you've shared a meal with the shugenja, you tell them you have to go to sleep. "I must get up before dawn," you say. "Can you tell me how to find the house of Mito Hitari?"

They consult among themselves before one of the monks says, "It is in the eastern sector, fourth ward, seventh block, where the second avenue meets the fifth cross-street."

You repeat the instructions until you've got them memorized, thank the shugenja for their hospitality, and say good night.

After a couple of hours of sleep, you're on your way back down the mountain to Kyoto. By the first rays of dawn, you're knocking on the door of the Hitari house. The rojo or house mistress, sees your monk's clothes, and asks politely what she can do for you. You decide to press your luck and ask if any visitors have arrived in the past day or two.

The rojo hesitates for a moment, then says, "Yes, a distant cousin of Lord Mito arrived yesterday."

"Could I see him?" you say boldly.

The rojo is taken aback, but she says, "I'll find out. Wait a moment."

Turn to page 74.

The ninja sits for a long while, saying nothing. Eventually you realize that he's meditating on what you've said. Finally he speaks. "I must admit that your story has the ring of truth. I must also admit that I have learned from it. It may be that I, too, have been under the influence of a vengeful *kami*.

"You see," he explains, "My family, the Hitari, is a branch of the Miyamotori. A long time ago— exactly one thousand years ago, in fact—my ancestor was unjustly sent into exile. He was the victim of the scheming of his brother, who had been promoted to a high rank, and did not want my ancestor as a rival. Sanchiro Miyamotori was the descendant of that scheming brother.

"Through all these centuries, our branch of the family has suffered in isolation. When I heard about the sword, I became convinced that if I could get it, I could redeem our lost honor. The sword and its power would be the foundation for my *ryu*. Through the *ryu*, my branch of the family would regain its prominence.

"Unfortunately, my brother got hold of the sword before I could. He sent it to your *dojo*, not only to spite me, but also to cause the destruction of your *dojo*. From what you say, his plan nearly worked.

"Now I can see that I've been in the grip of the angry *kami* of my ancestor. We two brothers have been repeating the mistake of our ancestors. Perhaps it is better, after all, that the sword is gone forever."

Turn to page 37.

Nada points her finger in the air. She has two sets of *shuko*—ninja claws—with her. You quickly put on one set. As you climb upward, you're pleased by how well the claws work on the wood of the walls. When you reach the top, you're amazed to see Nada punch a hole through the roof with her *shuko*. "I didn't know you could do that," you comment, as you follow her out the hole.

"Neither did I," she says.

You run along the top of the roof, leap into a tree, and climb down into the garden, from which you're able to escape into the city.

You lead Nada up the mountain toward the monastery. There you think you'll be able to find a safe place for the rituals required to return you and Nada to the present. On the way, you tell Nada how her grandmother helped you to come into the past, and ask her if she's figured out what the ninja really wanted.

"As you know," she answers, "he wanted the sword. I came into the past because I didn't have any choice, but also because I wanted to find out if his ancestor Mito really had been wrongly exiled. I hadn't found that out yet when you arrived, but if Mito acted anything like the ninja did, I'm sure he deserved what he got."

The End

60

It's foolish to draw the sword when you don't really know how to use it, you decide, and besides, you might damage the homing device. Keeping the sword sheathed, you slowly back up the trail. The two ninja advance, flanking you on either side.

"We told you to come alone!" one of them barks.

"I did," you respond. "Those men were reporters. They must have followed me. I didn't know they were here."

The ninja stop and eye you. "Are you Nada?"

"I'm her friend," you answer.

"That's the sword?"

"Yes."

"Put it down."

You set the sword on the ground. The ninja doing the talking comes forward to pick it up, while the other continues to advance on you, about to attack. Slowly you backpedal. When he gets closer, you pretend to lose your balance, and start to fall backward. He rushes you. Your feet suddenly fly out, planting a two-footed kick in his chest and knocking him flat on his back. You spring up, leap over him, and race down the path.

You arrive panting back at the post office, where Nada and Detective Jonsuro are waiting.

"They got the sword," you gasp. "Where's Yoshi?"

"We haven't seen him yet," Jonsuro says. "But the homing device is working."

Turn to page 72.

As Maki watches you finish your preparations, she reminds you that you have an important decision to make. "Before you go into the past, you must choose how you will disguise yourself," she says. "I suggest you dress as a Buddhist monk."

"Why not as a carpenter?" you ask. "When Nada and I went into the past before, we disguised ourselves as carpenters."

"You must remember that the aristocracy of the tenth century had no respect for working people. In the minds of the nobles, there was doubt as to whether common people were even human—and the nobles treated them as if they were not. The aristocracy would think nothing of abusing, enslaving, or even killing a laborer. But as a monk, you would be treated with some respect.

"That's true," you reply. "And no one would question my right to travel. But suppose I have to demonstrate my religious knowledge? If I disguise myself as a carpenter, I won't have to worry about that. Besides, I can always change my disguise."

"There are risks in either case," Maki says. "The choice is yours to make."

*If you decide to dress as a carpenter,
turn to page 50.*

*If you choose the monk disguise,
turn to page 20.*

62

You crouch and turn with the sword, wondering what will happen next. Suddenly you see out of the corner of your eye a black shape hurtling toward you. You swing the sword and cut the hurtling body cleanly in half, only to find it was a stuffed dummy.

Meanwhile, something grabs your foot. You try to move, but some kind of wire has pinned your foot to the ground. Suddenly the ninja springs up from a trapdoor covered in pine needles, laughing as you struggle to free your foot.

You hack at the wire, but every time you do, the ninja advances on you, and you have to keep him at bay with the sword. He pulls out a *shuriken*. Just as he whips it at you, your foot comes free, and you dive out of the way. You roll and spring to the ground, ready to take on the ninja.

You circle each other for what seems like hours, but neither of you can make a move on the other.

Finally you say, "I can see how much you want the sword. I'll hand it over to you if you show me Yoshi is safe."

"We trade at the same time?" the ninja asks.

"Right," you say.

He nods once, and motions for you to follow him. He leads you down a tiny footpath through the woods to a shack disguised in leaves and branches. The ninja calls to someone inside to bring out Yoshi.

Yoshi's face lights up when he sees you. "Are you all right?" you ask him.

"I'm okay," he says a little shakily.

Turn to page 43.

64

"Okay," you say to Nada, "let's get out of here. I'm sick of these reporters."

The two of you slip through a secret door in the hallway, and follow a passage that goes under the *dojo* and comes out in the woods a kilometer away. You walk to the nearest road and catch a bus to a friend's house. There you try to call Detective Jonsuro to let him know what you're doing, but the lines to the police station are busy all day.

"Probably the reporters," Nada says. "We'll have to wait until tomorrow. Meanwhile, what are we going to do about Yoshi?"

You and Nada think and think, but you can't come up with any ideas on Yoshi's kidnapping or why the ninja wants the sword. You call the Miyamotori family, whose ancestor was the original owner of the sword, but they don't want to get involved.

You get through to Detective Jonsuro the next morning. "I haven't found any leads," he says. "What about you?"

"Nothing," you say.

"We'll keep trying," he says grimly. "Meanwhile, I'm going to have a copy of the sword made. Can you tell me what it looked like?"

You and Nada describe the sword for him, and promise you'll call back at the end of the day.

Go on to the next page.

When you call again, you tell Jonsuro you don't know any more than you did that morning. "Neither do I," he confesses. "And we're out of time. Tomorrow is the day you're supposed to turn over the sword."

"I guess we'll just have to hope the fake sword works," you say.

"I'm having a homing device built into it," he says. "That may be our best chance for getting Yoshi back alive."

The next morning you and Nada meet Jonsuro at the police station. A throng of reporters still buzzes around the station, waiting for news.

As the detective drives you and Nada up to the village of Kanayama, you notice a car keeps reappearing behind you. "I think we're being followed," you say.

Turn to page 70.

66

"We'll give you the sword," you say quickly, "but it will take us a few days to get it. And when we give you the sword, you'll hand over Yoshi?"

"Correct," the ninja says.

"Where shall we make the exchange?"

"You will go to the mountain village of Kanayama," he instructs. "There is a telephone at the post office. It will ring at noon, three days from now. You will come absolutely alone. Believe me, I will know if you don't."

After you hang up, Nada blurts out, "Why did you do that? We don't have the sword!"

"I figured we could buy time by saying we'd give him the sword," you say. "At least now we know where he'll be in three days."

"Well," Jonsuro says, "I suppose that's better than nothing. But we don't have much to go on."

"Maybe we can make a copy of the sword," you suggest.

Nada shakes her head. "You remember that sword. It had great power. If the ninja's connected with it in any way, he'll recognize a fake immediately."

The detective leaves, saying he'll call you if he comes up with anything.

You manage to get a little rest, when the phone rings once again. Nada picks up the phone, and you watch her cringe as she listens. After she puts the phone down she tells you, "That was Yoshi's parents again. Somehow they heard about the sword. They said if we don't turn it over to the ninja, they'll have us put in jail."

Turn to page 92.

The ninja sees you a moment after you see him. He lets out a bloodcurdling scream, and rushes toward you. Your instincts take over. You roll at his feet, tripping him over the top of you. He springs back to his feet and jumps on you, and you both go rolling and wrestling down the hillside. You can feel that he's weak from the accident—but so are you.

You stop rolling just short of a rocky drop-off and separate. Getting shakily to your feet, you await his next attack. But he has disappeared. You look all around. There's no sign of him.

You crouch and wait, listening. For several minutes there's nothing but the sound of the woods. You decide that if you stay where you are, you'll be an easy target.

You have to move, but where? You could climb a tree. From there you'd have a better vantage point, and you'd also have gravity on your side if a chance came to attack the ninja.

On the other hand, your strength is gone. Maybe you should go back to the house for Nada. That may be just what he expects you to do, but you could take a roundabout route.

If you climb a tree to gain a better vantage point, turn to page 42.

If you start back toward the house, turn to page 83.

"Uh, I have to go get some more tools," you say as you back away from the three men squatting and eyeing you.

Just as you turn to leave, you step on a spot where the bark shingles have rotted through. They give way, and suddenly you're falling. A noblewoman at her mirror screams as you plunge into her room. You start to get up, thinking only about escaping. But you quickly realize you won't be going anywhere—not with two broken legs.

The End

70

Detective Jonsuro screeches into a U-turn and guns the car up a side road. He races through a dizzying series of turns that eventually bring you back onto the main road. The maneuver seems to have taken care of the car that was following you.

Jonsuro stops just outside the town of Kana-yama a few minutes before noon. Taking the sword out of the trunk, he points to a tiny jewel on the hilt. "That's the homing device," he says, handing the sword to you. "Good luck."

Alone, you walk through the village to the post office. You're startled to see the car that had been tailing you parked nearby. But you have no time to worry about it now.

Exactly at noon the telephone rings. You pick it up. "Go to the north end of the village. A path leads into the woods and up the mountain." Click.

You do as you're instructed. The path climbs steeply through the woods. Then, suddenly, you hear two cries from below. You run down the path. Turning a corner, you nearly trip over two figures crumpled on the ground, victims of ninja daggers. And right in front of you are two ninja!

You recognize the victims as two of the reporters who have been following the kidnapping story—a little too closely, it seems.

Your first impulse is to run. But then you remember you have the sword. Even though you haven't studied much *kendo*, or swordsmanship, your skills might be good enough to hold them off.

If you draw the sword, turn to page 106.

If you think you'd better not, turn to page 60.

"How can I get this ninja to Nada's grand-mother's house?" you wonder out loud.

"Let's put him in a trunk!" a student suggests.

The class helps you to tie up the ninja with all the knots you can think of, load him into a trunk, and lock it tightly. When the taxi arrives, you explain to the driver, "I need to get this trunk to my grand-mother's house. It's a big fare. The house is three hours away. I'll pay you double what's on the meter—and a big tip."

This makes the driver happy. He helps you lash the trunk to the roof. You thank your students, and you're on your way.

Everything goes smoothly until you're on the final steep mountain grade to Nada's grand-mother's house. The trunk begins shaking violently back and forth on the roof. The ninja has woken up and is trying to break out!

"What's going on here?" the driver demands.

You try to act innocent. "What do you mean?"

"That does it," the driver says. He pulls over to the side of the road and, leaving the engine running, jumps out to look at the trunk.

You eye the steering wheel. Should you jump into the front seat and drive away? You've had some driving lessons, and you figure if you drive fast enough you might make it to the house before the ninja breaks free. But you could also try to convince the taxi driver to keep going instead.

If you decide to drive yourself,
turn to page 78.

If you try to talk to the driver, turn to page 90.

Detective Jonsuro takes you into the back of the post office where his men have set up a tracking table to follow the sword. You watch as they plot the course of the homing device up the mountain. Near the top it abruptly stops. Jonsuro points to the map and says, "There's a temple right there. We'll give them twenty minutes to free Yoshi. Then we go after them."

The twenty minutes pass slowly. Yoshi does not appear, and the sword does not move. "Let's go!" the detective orders.

You and Nada follow Jonsuro and his officers back up the path. After a long climb, you finally reach the temple shown on the map. The police officers spread out for an assault on the temple. Jonsuro addresses the inhabitants through a megaphone, telling them they have two minutes to surrender. There's no answer.

Jonsuro motions to his officers, and they move in on the temple, their guns drawn. They kick in the front and back doors simultaneously and rush inside. A few minutes later, an officer reappears at the front door. "There's no one here," he announces.

You, Nada, and Jonsuro go into the temple. The sword has been driven into the floor. A note is stuck on the blade.

"It is unfortunate for Yoshi," the note reads, *"that you chose to give me a fake. You were warned."*

You wonder how you're going to explain this to Yoshi's parents.

The End

74

The *rojo* returns and shows you in. "He asked that you wait for him back here," she says, leading you through the house to a small room in a far corner of the mansion.

The *rojo* leaves and you wait uncomfortably for the cousin to show up. As the wait goes on, you begin to suspect you're being set up. But then the *rojo* appears with a pot of tea, saying, "My lord apologizes for his lateness. He will be in to see you very soon."

You start sipping the tea, wondering if you should get out while you can. Then suddenly you stop drinking. The tea smells unusual, and you start to feel strange.

You've stepped into a trap, and there's only one way out. In an exaggerated motion you stand up, wobble on your feet, and then collapse, breaking the teacup on the floor. You just hope you haven't already drunk enough poison that you will soon collapse altogether.

It takes only a few seconds for someone to appear. He drags you out of the room and down a corridor. You can tell by his strength that he must be a ninja. The only thing you have going for you is the element of surprise—as Nada has told you before, with it you can defeat a much stronger enemy.

Go on to the next page.

You hear a sliding door open. The ninja grabs you, lifts you up underneath your arms, and takes you through the door in front of him, propping you up with his body. Suddenly you feel cold steel against your neck, and he says with triumph, "I think things have changed now, Nada."

At the same moment as you hear Nada's sharp intake of breath, you stomp on the ninja's foot and simultaneously knock his knife arm back with your elbow. He's caught completely off guard, and this gives Nada the opening she needs. She leaps, and pins him to the floor with a single move. You work fast, tearing your monk's robes into strips and using them to tie the ninja up—but not fast enough. He screams for help.

The sound of footsteps comes from every direction. You look at Nada, silently asking, "Which way?"

Turn to page 59.

76

"Okay," you say to Basho, "we'll take the fire approach. How do you plan to set your trap?"

"Wait here," Basho says. He runs off, and returns with a *kyoketsu shoge*, a rope with a steel ring at the end.

"You go in first," Basho tells you, "and draw the intruder out. We'll wait back here, and when he attacks you, we'll spring the trap on him."

You go along with Basho's plan, doubtful that it will work. You walk into the house, open and unguarded. To your surprise, you're immediately flattened by some immense force from above. You quickly realize the intruder is a ninja, an incredibly strong one, and he's got you pinned to the floor.

Then Basho and the other students burst in. Basho throws the ring, knocking the ninja on the head. He grabs the ring, but the other students hold him back, and Basho wraps him up with the rope. This gives you a chance to apply a nerve pinch that leaves the ninja unconscious.

Now you've got a ninja on your hands, and you have no idea what to do with him. You have to act quickly because, once he comes to, you doubt you'll be able to keep him under control.

You wish Nada was here. But since her grandmother has no phone, the only way to reach her would be to go up to her grandmother's, with the ninja in tow. It might be easier just to turn him over to the police.

If you call the police, turn to page 55.

If you want to go to Nada's grandmother's house, turn to page 71.

78

You leap into the driver's seat, put the car in gear, and take off. The taxi driver's yells fade behind you as you accelerate. But the trunk is shaking madly back and forth. The movement is rocking the car, and you can't keep a grip on the steering wheel. As you screech around a bend you lose control. The car rolls, flipping over once and landing upright again.

You look out your window just in time to see the trunk, having broken loose from the roof, tumble over the edge of the road and down the mountain ravine.

You're bruised and bleeding, but you manage to drive the rest of the way to Nada's grandmother's house. "What happened?" Nada cries when you stumble in the door.

You tell her, finishing with the sight of the trunk careening down the ravine. "I don't see how he could have survived," you say, still a little in shock.

"The important thing is to take care of you," Nada says. She makes you lie down, and dresses your wounds.

"What about your grandmother?" you ask, noticing a sleeping figure in the next room. "How is she?"

"She'll pull through," Nada says. "It's strange, though. I think it was a ninja poison that was making her sick. Luckily, I knew the antidote."

Go on to the next page.

You rest for a little while, but then you remember the car. "I've got to go find the taxi driver," you call to Nada, hobbling toward the door.

"You've got to go to a hospital," Nada replies firmly. "But I'll take you. I'll be out to the car in a minute."

You open the door and step outside. Darkness has fallen. Looking idly into the dark woods, your eye picks up a shape moving in the trees. You go to have a closer look. Suddenly, with a sharp intake of breath, you see the ninja, battered and bloody, trudging up the hill toward you!

Turn to page 67.

80

The next morning Nada and Detective Jonsuro show up at the *dojo*. You tell Nada the whole story. She tells you that her grandmother was sick because she was being poisoned. "It was a ninja poison," Nada says. "I was able to counteract it. But I suspect the real purpose for the poisoning was to draw me away from the *dojo* so that the ninja could attack."

At that moment the phone rings. You pick it up. "Hello?"

A muffled voice says, "Do you want Yoshi back alive?"

"Yes, of course," you reply.

"Then give me the sword," the voice says.

"What sword?"

"You know what I'm talking about," the voice replies savagely. The line goes dead.

Nada and Jonsuro watch as you put down the receiver. "It was the kidnapper. He said he wanted the sword."

"What sword?" Jonsuro asks.

"I wonder if he means the sword that was sent to the *dojo* last year," you muse.

"That must be it," Nada says. "We never did find out where the sword came from. Maybe it was stolen from him."

"Where's the sword now?" the detective asks.

Go on to the next page.

"It's gone," Nada says, "and there's no way to get it back."

Before she can go on, the phone rings again. You pick it up slowly as the other two watch.

The sound of Yoshi's voice tears at you. "Don't worry, I'm all right—" he says, before the muffled voice comes on the line and demands, "I want the sword—now!"

You wonder if you should buy time by telling the ninja he can have the sword. Or should you try to explain that the sword is gone forever?

If you say you'll give him the sword,
turn to page 66.

If you tell him the sword is gone,
turn to page 87.

It's best to try to get help from Nada, you think, as you climb the hill. You don't want to go straight to the house, so you traverse the hillside, circling around to the other side of the house, before continuing up. All the while your ears are pricked for any sound that might give away the ninja's presence. But he seems to be nowhere near.

You approach the top of the hill, and see the welcome light from the house only thirty yards away. You start to call out to Nada, but then you do hear a sound—the crunch of tires on gravel. Suddenly the taxicab comes barreling over the edge of the hill, right at you. You're frozen in surprise. The last thing you see is the grille of the car.

The End

84

Once you have the ninja laid out and tied up in the house, you come back out to look for the driver. But apparently he's decided he's had enough—both he and the taxi are gone.

Back inside, you ask Nada how her grandmother is.

"Well, it's interesting," she says. "She's recovering. But I figured out that she was being poisoned. Not only that, it was a ninja poison."

"But why?" you wonder. "Was it to draw you away from the *dojo*?"

"Yes," Nada says. "And it must have been the work of this fellow we've got tied up here. Tomorrow we'll turn the tables on him and find out what this is all about. But for now I think we all need some rest."

The next morning you meet Nada's grandmother, Maki. She appears to be feeling much better. "Shall we start?" she says briskly.

You watch with fascination as she mixes an herb drink. "This will prepare him for *saiminjutsu*," she explains. You know from what Nada has taught you that *saiminjutsu* is a form of ninja hypnotism.

Maki feeds the ninja the potion as he begins to regain consciousness. Soon his eyes become glazed. Maki's magical *kuji* hand-signs then put him under hypnosis.

Go on to the next page.

"What were you doing at the *dojo*?" she asks.

"The sword," the ninja says dreamily. "The sword of the Miyamotori. My sword."

"The one that was sent to the *dojo* last year!" you exclaim.

"Why did you want the sword?" Maki prompts.

"Its power—we have waited a thousand years to start our own *ryu*, and avenge our family . . . ."

"What happened to your family?"

"My ancestor was sent into exile. But with the sword, I will avenge him."

Maki draws you and Nada into another room. "I sense the presence of a *kami,* a spirit," she says, "but an evil one. It may even be the *kami* of this ancestor of his who was sent into exile. Where is the sword he's talking about?"

"We no longer have it," Nada says. "It was destroying the *dojo.*"

Turn to page 51.

86

You call the class to attention and say, "I must go into the house for a few moments. Continue with your exercises and wait for me to come back."

You slip into the house, and, employing *onshin-jutsu,* you investigate every corner of the house—the basement, the roof, even the secret compartments and trapdoors. You find nothing, but you sense someone was there.

When you go back outside, several students run toward you, crying, "Come quick! Help!"

You race back to the training grounds. "Someone kidnapped Yoshi," a student says breathlessly. "We didn't notice until it was too late. A man just came out of the trees and grabbed him. We heard Yoshi cry out, and we ran after him, but they both disappeared."

"Can you describe the kidnapper?" you ask, trying to contain the panicky feeling spreading inside you.

"He was dressed in black," another student says. "I think he was a ninja."

Oh, no, you think. Your first day alone at the *dojo,* and one of the students is kidnapped by a ninja!

But there's no time for feeling sorry. You hesitate for a moment, trying to decide whether you should go inside and call the police, or whether you should chase after the kidnapper immediately.

If you decide to call the police, turn to page 91.

If you ask the students which way the ninja went, turn to page 107.

"We don't have the sword," you say. "It's, gone."

"You're lying," the ninja replies flatly.

"Let me explain," you plead. "If you mean the sword that once belonged to Sanchiro Miyamotori, it was sent to us anonymously last year, and—"

"I know it was sent to you last year," he interrupts icily.

"Well, then, who sent it?"

There's a moment of hesitation before he answers, "My brother sent it. But it is rightfully mine."

"Why did your brother send it to us?"

"That is none of your concern," the ninja explodes. "I demand that you return the sword to me."

"Why do you say it is yours?" you insist. "Are you a Miyamotori?"

"Yes! No!" His voice quavers. "Give me back the sword!"

"The sword is gone," you say gently. "There's no way to get it back."

"I don't believe you."

"I'll tell you the whole story," you propose. "Let's meet and talk."

"No!" Detective Jonsuro blurts out behind you. "It's too dangerous!"

"Who's with you?" the ninja demands.

If you ignore Jonsuro and again propose a meeting, turn to page 27.

If you heed the detective's warning, turn to page 95.

Nada helps you back to the house. Your body hurts everywhere. Nada dresses your old wounds again, plus the new ones. "That will have to do for tonight," she says. "Try to get some sleep. I'll go for help in the morning."

You close your eyes as Nada stands up to turn off the light. Suddenly the sound of the window smashing jolts your eyes open. The ninja stands before you, bloodier than ever, a crazed look in his eye. Nada is on the floor next to the window.

You're too stunned to move. As the ninja raises a knife to throw at you, you feel you can only accept the end.

Then the ninja just crumples to the ground. Behind him you see Nada's grandmother, applying the death grip to his neck. She looks almost as dazed as you do, but, looking down at the ninja, she manages to explain, "I had no choice. Even before he returned, I'd woken up and I could feel his rage. My *sakki* told me it was the same rage that had tried to poison me. It was so powerful, I could do nothing else."

You nod in agreement, and lead Nada's grandmother back to the room.

The End

90

You jump out of the taxi and grab the driver. "Listen to me," you say, fixing him with your eyes. "There's a ninja in that trunk, and if you don't get us to where we're headed as fast as you can, he'll kill both of us."

The driver can tell you're serious. The two of you get back into the taxi, and he puts the pedal to the floor. The trunk is shaking so violently you think it might cause the car to turn over. But the driver is good, and he somehow manages to keep the taxi on the road, screeching around the mountain curves as fast as he can.

At last you reach the long dirt driveway leading to Nada's grandmother's house. But just as you pull in, something punches through the roof of the car. A hand armed with *shuko* tears at the air between you and the driver. The steel claws hook on to the driver's collar and shake him violently. As you open your door to jump out, the driver loses control of the car. It crashes into a tree. You're tossed out, hitting the ground with a roll.

Nada runs from the house as you pop back onto your feet. The ninja's *shuko* continues to shake the driver back and forth. You get back into the car, grab the ninja's wrist, and twist it. Nada jumps onto the roof and pries open the trunk. Once you get the claws out of the driver's collar, you continue to hold on to the ninja's wrist, hoping it will give Nada a chance to knock him unconscious again. Finally the wrist goes limp as Nada gives the ninja a hard crack on the neck. "Help me drag him inside the house," she calls.

Turn to page 84.

You run back into the house and call the police, asking them to block off all the roads in the area. The police tell you to get all the other students inside the *dojo* and stay there until they arrive.

You follow instructions and soon some police officers arrive. A man in an overcoat walks over to you. "I'm Detective Jonsuro," the man says. "What happened?"

You go over every detail of the incident, and Jonsuro asks, "Do you have any idea who this ninja is? Why would someone want to kidnap Yoshi?"

"I don't know," you say.

"We'll talk to Yoshi's family," the detective says. "Maybe the kidnapper wants ransom from them."

"I doubt that's the case," you comment.

"Why?" the detective asks sharply.

"I'm not sure," you have to admit. "It's just a feeling."

"Well, stay at the *dojo* until we get back to you," he instructs.

"What about Nada?" you say.

"We'll contact her at her grandmother's," Jonsuro promises.

Once all the police officers leave, there's nothing for you to do but wait. You hear nothing for the rest of the day, but in the evening Yoshi's father calls. "If you don't get Yoshi back safely, we'll see to it that your *dojo* is closed down," his father says.

"I'll do my best," you try to assure him. But you go to bed feeling very depressed.

Turn to page 80.

92

The next morning things get worse. Headlines like NINJA KIDNAPPING are spread all over the front pages of the newspapers.

Soon the phone is ringing off the hook, and reporters are buzzing the doorbell. They ask you over and over again to describe the kidnapping. They want to know all about the sword, and your activities at the *dojo,* and whether you're involved in a blood feud with another ninja clan. Afraid they'll find out you no longer have the sword, you and Nada tell the reporters as little as you can. When they ask if the kidnapper has called, you say, "No comment."

The stream of reporters, photographers, and television cameras seems to have no end. Everyone repeatedly asks you questions about how you feel. Finally, late in the afternoon, you get a moment alone with Nada in the kitchen. "I can't take much more of this," you say wearily.

"Well," Nada says thoughtfully, "we don't have to if we don't want to."

"They won't leave us alone just because we ask them to," you inform her.

"That's not what I meant," Nada replies. "This is our chance. We could slip into the secret passageways under the house, and hide out until it's time to meet the kidnapper."

---

*If you agree with Nada's suggestion,
turn to page 64.*

*If you think it's a bad idea to hide out,
turn to page 98.*

94

At the lord's mansion, the house master has a long list of tasks for you. "First you can fix the roof. Then we want you to rebuild the wing where the second and third wives live, and then the pagoda in the garden." Seeing the look of dismay on your face, he says, "Don't worry. I'll give you three laborers to help. And you'll be well paid for your work."

You don't know what to do, except get to work on the roof and hope for a chance to make a getaway. You take your three helpers up to the roof, but quickly realize you're in trouble. The men are waiting expectantly for your instructions, and you know next to nothing about the building techniques of the time.

Turn to page 69.

"I *can't* meet with you," you say, following Detective Jonsuro's warning.

"Of course you can't meet me," the ninja replies acidly. "You know that I will see through your lie. You have the sword, and I want it!"

The phone is slammed down in your ear. You turn to Nada and Jonsuro. "What now? He's more convinced than ever that we have the sword."

"We'll give him a fake," the detective says. "Unless we can catch him first. He'll call again, and when he does, tell him you'll give up the sword."

The ninja does call again, the next day. "This is your last chance," he says.

"All right," you say, trying to sound defeated. "You can have the sword."

He gives you the location of a mountain temple where you are to leave the sword. "If you do everything correctly," he concludes, "Yoshi will be waiting for you in the village post office."

Jonsuro has a sword manufactured from the description you give him. The next day he drives you and Nada up to a village near the temple. You take the fake sword into the temple alone. No one appears to be there. You leave the sword, and return to the village, hoping to find Yoshi. He's not there. You wait all day with Nada and Jonsuro, but Yoshi never appears.

The next day, the ninja calls again. "I don't need fakes," the ninja says angrily.

You never hear from him—or Yoshi—again.

The End

You do as instructed, hiking up the steep path through a dense forest. The trail takes you higher and higher, until, two hours later, you turn a corner and suddenly come upon a small temple in a clearing. Just as suddenly, you're surrounded by three black-clad ninja.

The ninja escort you into the temple, where a small, somber man is seated on a pillow. He motions for you to sit down. The ninja leave.

"You were wise to come alone," he comments. "Now, tell me what you say has become of my sword."

You tell him the whole story, finishing with the discovery that the sword had inflamed the vengeful *kami* of Sanchiro Miyamotori, which tried to destroy the *dojo*.

"The most obvious solution," you conclude, "was for us to placate the *kami* and get rid of the sword."

Turn to page 57.

98

"Hiding out's not such a good idea," you say to Nada. "We might miss something important if we leave."

"Whatever you say," Nada sighs.

You spend the rest of the day fending off reporters, and finally, after everyone has left, you lock the door and try to get some sleep. Early the next morning, you're jarred from a fitful sleep by a loud ringing.

"Hello," you say wearily into the telephone.

The static on the line tells you the call is international. "Nada Kurayama?" the man on the other end inquires.

"She's asleep," you say. "Can I help you?"

The man sounds guarded. "I've heard about the kidnapping case. I have some information that may be of assistance to you."

This wakes you up. "What is it?"

"I understand the kidnapper wants a certain sword, a sword that once belonged to the Miyamotori family."

"Go on," you urge.

"If that is correct, I know who the kidnapper is."

You wait for the man to continue.

"And I know where he is."

"Where?" you ask, a little skeptical.

Go on to the next page.

"I will tell you on one condition: When he is arrested, give him this message from his brother—tell him, 'This is the revenge of Taro.' If you promise to do that, I will tell you exactly where to find him."

Figuring you have nothing to lose, you say, "All right."

"Above the village of Kanayama there is a mountain. A path leads to a small temple on the mountain, a mile above the village. A complex of secret rooms is under the temple. You can get into the rooms through a trapdoor hidden underneath the cryptomeria tree to the west of the temple. You'll find my brother there. Don't forget the message."

After putting down the phone, you wake up Nada and call Detective Jonsuro. "It's probably a crank call," Jonsuro says tiredly, "but we'd better check it out, anyway."

Turn to page 108.

100

Silently you approach the building. Something at the entrance catches your eye: a piece of white cloth dangling on a nail. You realize it's a piece torn from Yoshi's robe!

You touch the cloth thoughtfully and continue into the house, your ears attuned to any sound. All you hear is the wind whistling through the windows. All you see is dust in the rays of the setting sun. Then you spot another bit of white cloth at the foot of a staircase. It's just like the piece you found on the nail. You look up the dark stairs, unable to see where they lead.

All of a sudden you wonder if the bits of cloth weren't a little too easy to find. Maybe the ninja *wants* you to come up the stairs—maybe he's waiting for you at the top. You wonder if you should go outside and see if there's another way to get up to the second floor.

On the other hand, you're receiving no sense of danger coming from the top of the stairs from your *sakki,* and you're reluctant to go back outside when you seem to be so close to finding Yoshi.

If you go up the stairs, turn to page 105.

If you go back outside, turn to page 110.

102

Yoshi seems hardly to be breathing. You pat his cheek, trying to bring him to consciousness. Slowly he comes around. He looks at you foggily, barely recognizing you. You think the ninja must have drugged him.

When Yoshi is able to respond to your questions, you check to make sure no bones are broken. You help him to his feet, but he sways woozily, and you notice an abrasion on the side of his head. Whether his wooziness is from having been drugged or from a possible concussion, you realize he won't be able to walk by himself.

You don't want to let the ninja go, but you have no choice. You must get Yoshi to a hospital. Perhaps later you'll have a chance to unravel the reasons behind Yoshi's kidnapping, and track down the ninja. But right now, a long, hard, night trip back to the *dojo* lies ahead of you.

The End

For a tense half hour you and Nada wait in silence. Outside, men shout, and the light of torches flickers through the partition.

Finally, however, all is quiet again. You poke your head out the window and whisper, "I think they've moved on." You nod your thanks to the couple inside, and begin climbing out. "Good luck," the man whispers to you.

You and Nada escape back through the garden and into the deserted western sector of the city, where Nada has a chance to tell you what happened.

"The idea was that Hitari and I would come into the past to find out exactly why his ancestor Mito was exiled. But we ran into you before we had a chance."

"Does that mean we still have to find out?" you ask.

"We can do that in a library—in the present," Nada says. "Right now, I want to get as far away from Hitari as I can."

The End

Vowing to be extra cautious, you take your first step up the stairs. Slowly, making no sound, pausing at each stair to listen, you ascend, your eyes fixed on the darkness above for any sign of movement.

Halfway up the staircase, your foot comes down gently on one of the steps. You put your full weight on the step and hear a splintering sound. Suddenly the board gives way, and your leg falls through. You grasp for something to hold on to, but the whole staircase seems to be collapsing. You tumble down to the floor below, wood and mortar crashing on top of you.

When all the crashing is over, you find yourself unable to move, buried underneath a pile of beams and boards. Even if you manage to get free somehow, Yoshi and the ninja will be long gone.

The End

106

You don't know much about *kendo,* but you think you can fake it. You use the sky-to-ground movement to draw the sword, and let out a blood-curdling yell at the same time.

To your surprise, a look of terror comes into the eyes of the ninja. They run screaming into the woods. At first you think you must have done a good acting job, but then you remember that the sword is reputed to have fantastic powers, and that must have frightened them.

You're not sure what to do next, so you decide just to keep going. You continue up the trail, sword drawn, ready for attack from any side, your ears attuned to the slightest sounds.

Then a voice speaks to you, loud and clear, as if someone is right next to you. You recognize it as the voice on the telephone—the voice of the ninja. "Give me the sword," he says, "and I will spare your life."

You look all around—in the trees, on the ground, everywhere—to see where he could be hiding. But your trained eyes find nothing.

"This is your last chance," the voice says. "If you want to live."

You stop, and stand very still, sword raised, attuning to *sakki,* the presence of the killer.

In a flash you whip the sword around to your left and above your head in the spinning-sword movement. It slices a falling branch in half—a split second before the branch would have hit your head.

The voice laughs. "Very good," the ninja says. "I see the sword still has its power."

Turn to page 62.

"Which way did they go?" you ask.

The students point you in the direction of the deep wooded hillside, and you take off after the ninja. The ninja leaves very few signs of his flight, but you're still able to follow him using ninja tracking methods.

The tracks lead in an unexpected direction. They take you into the hills, higher and higher, toward the mountains to the east. You pursue the ninja relentlessly, up through forests and meadows, but still you don't catch sight of him or Yoshi.

The sun sinks toward the horizon. Your legs ache and your lungs burn. Coming up over the crest of a steep ridge, you suddenly stop dead in your tracks.

You're in a clearing. A broken-down building of some kind sits in the center of the clearing. It looks like it may have been a lodging house at one time. Now it's overgrown with weeds, and the windows are broken and burned out.

You scour the area around the clearing looking for signs of the ninja, but there are none. The vacant building appears to be the only place he could have gone.

Turn to page 100.

108

Four hours later you and Nada are following Jonsuro and his officers up a mountain path above the village of Kanayama. The trail climbs steeply, then suddenly crests on a clearing, in the middle of which sits a small temple. Jonsuro's officers retreat back down the trail a little way while you and Nada look for the trapdoor.

"It's right where the caller said it would be," you report to Jonsuro when you return.

"Okay. Here's the plan," Jonsuro says. "My men will storm the place through the trapdoor. You, Nada, and I will cover the temple, in case anyone tries to escape that way."

You and Nada creep into the temple with Jonsuro and hide while you wait for the police team to attack. A sudden burst of fighting sounds comes from below. Then all is quiet.

You wait for movement from underneath the temple. Sure enough, a trapdoor opens in the floor. You prepare to spring—then you see Yoshi!

"You're safe!" you cry, running to hug him.

"When I heard the sound of people coming in, I used my training to escape from the two men who were guarding me," he explains.

You take him out of the temple and wait down on the trail. A few minutes later Jonsuro joins you. "There were four of them down there," he says. "Every single one committed *seppuku*. I guess they saw they couldn't escape arrest."

"Well, we may never know what this has all been about," you say, "but we got Yoshi back, and that's good enough."

The End

110

You back out of the house slowly and soundlessly, wary now of traps that may be waiting for you. Outside, you circle around the house and find a vine growing up the back wall. You shinny up the vine to reach a second-floor window, and pull yourself inside.

You crouch beneath the window and listen. There are no sounds. Slowly and carefully you begin to investigate. In one of the rooms you find signs that the dust has been disturbed. Looking closer, you can make out fresh footprints.

Just then you hear a muffled cry from downstairs, followed by running steps. You start for the stairs, but think better of it, and return to the window through which you entered. You climb out, and as you begin to slide down the vine, a figure turns the corner below you.

Without hesitation, you leap, pushing off from the side of the house. In midair, you realize you're about to hit Yoshi, for the ninja is carrying him over his shoulders! You twist, trying to soften the impact, and hit a glancing blow with your feet off the ninja's thigh. He tumbles to the ground, and Yoshi flips over the ninja's head.

The ninja bounces back to his feet. Yoshi lies motionless on the ground. You and the ninja eye each other for a moment, then you spring at him. He flees into the brush. You start to give chase, but quickly turn back to see if Yoshi is all right.

Turn to page 102.

112

You want to have all your senses to deal with the intruder, so you don't use the earplugs.

Soon you're hearing sounds from all over the house. First there's knocking at the front door, then pounding on the roof, then noises from the back. The sounds increase in volume and intensity until the whole house is shaking wildly. It seems as if the house is going to come apart.

The sounds are driving you mad. Finally you realize you must get out of the house and escape the noise. You make a dash for one of the entrances to a network of secret passageways, where at least you'll be protected from a sneak attack.

But as you head for the secret door, you catch sight of a blur coming at you. Your reflexes are slow. Suddenly you're in the viselike grip of a ninja. Now you'll never have a chance to find out what this is all about.

The End

ABOUT THE AUTHOR

JAY LEIBOLD was born in Denver, Colorado. He is the author of many books in the Choose Your Own Adventure series, including *Secret of the Ninja*, the sequels *Return of the Ninja* and *The Lost Ninja*, *You Are a Millionaire*, *Revenge of the Russian Ghost*, and *Fight for Freedom*. He lives in San Francisco, where he plays catcher and first base for the Creeping Terror softball team. He is currently at work on a new series.

ABOUT THE ILLUSTRATOR

FRANK BOLLE studied at Pratt Institute. He has worked as an illustrator for many national magazines and now creates and draws cartoons for magazines as well. He has also worked in advertising and children's educational materials and has drawn and collaborated on several newspaper comic strips, including *Annie* and *Winnie Winkle*. He has illustrated many books in the Choose Your Own Adventure series, including *Master of Kung Fu*, *Return of the Ninja*, *Through the Black Hole*, *The Worst Day of Your Life*, *Master of Tae Kwon Do*, *Hijacked!*, *Master of Karate*, *Invaders From Within*, *The Lost Ninja*, *Daredevil Park*, and *Kidnapped!* A native of Brooklyn Heights, New York, Mr. Bolle now lives and works in Westport, Connecticut.